Produced by Mega-Books of New York, Inc.
Design and Art Direction by Michaelis/Carpelis Design Assoc.

Cover illustration: Ken Spencer

SOARING
SUMMER

by Ann Richards

interior illustrations by
Frank Mayo

STECK-VAUGHN
C O M P A N Y

Chapter One

"Esther! Wake up!" Philip Li shook his older sister's shoulder. "We're coming to our stop!"

"Okay, okay," Esther said in a sleepy voice. She rubbed her eyes and looked out the bus window. They sure were far from home. The bus was driving through a heavily wooded area. Farther off, the mountain tops were glistening with snow.

"It's so beautiful!" Esther thought. Then she caught herself. She had forgotten she was mad at her parents for making her come here. She didn't want to spend the summer with her kid brother and her older cousin, Martin Wang. She wanted to be with her friends, rollerblading and playing sports at the local teen center.

Esther had only half listened when her mother explained what Martin's job was. It had something to do with birds.

She barely knew her cousin and Esther didn't like the idea of "roughing it" with him and her little brother.

Still, she couldn't help feeling drawn to the beautiful scenery.

The bus pulled into a gas station.

"There he is!" yelled Philip. He hopped off the bus as it came to a stop. A green pickup truck drove towards them down a bumpy dirt road.

Esther and Philip waved. Martin honked the horn in greeting. He pulled up next to them. "Welcome to the great outdoors! Toss your bags in back and jump in," he called out the window.

They swung their bags into the open

back of the truck and climbed into the
front seat.

"So, you two, how was the trip?"
asked Martin in a friendly voice.

"Great!" said Philip, answering for
both of them.

Esther kept quiet. This trip was fine
for Philip since he had nothing better to
do. She, however, wanted to be back in
the city.

But her parents had explained that was impossible.

Mr. and Mrs. Li and Esther had come to the United States from China twelve years ago, just before Philip was born.

Her parents worked in a relative's florist shop. After ten years of hard work and saving every penny, Mr. and Mrs. Li opened their own business in the suburbs. Now it was their turn to help other relatives.

Esther was proud of her parents. But she was still angry about having to give up her room for the summer. Some cousins she had never even met would stay there until they could find their own place.

Esther gazed out the truck window. She saw a huge bird soaring in the sky. Philip saw it, too. He leaned over Esther to get a better view.

"Hey!" Esther said, pushing Philip away. "Give me some space, all right?"

"Look!" Philip ignored his sister. "It's an eagle!"

Martin glanced up to where Philip was pointing. "Close. But actually, that's a hawk."

"How can you tell?" asked Philip.

"Eagles are bigger than hawks, and their wings are shaped differently," said Martin. Now Esther began to remember what her parents had said about her cousin. Martin was an expert on eagles. He worked with the Wildlife Research Center. His job was to tag young eagles and keep track of them.

"Well, whatever kind of bird it is," Philip said, excited by the sighting, "it sure is cool!"

Esther disagreed. Bird-watching was about the farthest thing from cool she could think of.

Chapter Two

After about an hour's drive on unpaved roads, Martin pulled onto an even rougher road. He switched into four-wheel drive. The truck bounced along for another twenty minutes.

Esther was beginning to feel carsick. She wished they would hurry up and get there.

"We're almost home," said Martin, as if he were reading her mind.

A few minutes later, Martin pulled up in front of a small cabin. A picnic table and benches stood outside next to a circle of stones surrounding the ashes of a campfire.

Martin jumped out of the truck and grabbed their bags from the back. Philip scurried out of the driver's side as Esther slowly got out of the truck. Her legs had cramped up during the ride. She shook them out and stretched.

"What's that?" asked Philip. He pointed to a small building the size of a large closet, several yards from the small cabin.

"That's the outhouse," answered Martin. He walked over and pushed open the door. A strong smell drifted toward Esther.

"Gross!" she cried.

"Well, you've got to go somewhere," Martin said with a smile. "It's really not so bad once you get used to it."

"I'll never get used to this," Esther mumbled to herself.

She followed Martin and Philip into the cabin. It was divided into two rooms by a sheet hanging from the ceiling.

Each room had a cot and a small table made from an old wooden crate. There was a sink under the window. It was so depressing that Esther's eyes began to tear up with disappointment. She had imagined a cozy cottage in the woods, with a brick fireplace and soft, overstuffed furniture.

"You two will sleep here," said Martin, dropping their bags onto the floor. "I'll sleep outside in a tent."

Philip looked around the bare cabin. "Where's all your stuff?" he asked.

"I don't have much. My tools are in the truck and I have a change of clothes in my backpack," said Martin. "When you're on the go the way I am, it's easier to travel light," he added, eyeing Esther's heavy bag.

Martin and Philip went back outside. Esther stretched out on her cot. She closed her eyes and a pleasant sleepy feeling washed over her.

"It's an eagle!" Philip's cry woke her right back up. Esther sighed and went outside to see what was going on.

"I can't see a thing," Esther said.

"Here," said Martin. He offered her his binoculars.

She took them and adjusted the focus. What had been a speck in the sky was now clearly a big, beautiful bird.

"What's it doing?" asked Esther.

"It's hunting," her brother replied.

"What can it catch all the way up there? Airplanes?" Esther sneered.

"Actually, its prey is on the ground," explained Martin. "Eagles have excellent eyesight—about eight times better than ours. An eagle spots its prey from very high in the air."

"Then it folds its wings and swoops down," added Philip. "At the last

moment it opens its wings and thrusts its feet forward. Then it strikes!" He pushed his hands toward Esther's face with his fingers bent like claws. She swatted them away.

Some summer vacation—watching eagles all day. It would be the longest eight weeks of Esther's life!

Chapter Three

Martin woke Esther and Philip at dawn. After a quick breakfast of pancakes and eggs, they were in the truck and rolling. About an hour later, Martin pulled over to the side of the road.

"There's a nest up in the mountains I want to check out," Martin said as they got out of the truck. "Some eagles made it last year, and I want to see if they returned to it this year."

There was no trail. Martin led the way through the thick woods. "By the way," he said, casually, "there are bears in these woods."

Esther stopped walking.

"Don't worry. It's rare for bears to attack people," Martin added. "Mostly, they'll leave you alone. But if you see one, just try to get out of its way nice and slow. Don't run or it will chase you."

"Great!" Esther thought as they continued up the steep mountainside. Playing tag with a bear wasn't her idea of fun.

Sweat was pouring off Esther's forehead as the climb grew steeper. She stopped to take off her jacket and stuff it into her day pack. When she started walking again, she crashed right into Philip, who was crouched behind Martin.

"What is it?" she asked in a tense voice. Thoughts of bears crowded her mind.

"Look through those branches," whispered Martin.

Esther strained her eyes and saw

something that looked like a deer, only larger—much larger.

"That's an elk," said Martin. "You can tell it's a male by its antlers."

The animal must have sensed their presence because it turned and bounded away.

"Wow!" said Philip.

Even Esther was impressed by the majestic animal.

Finally the trio reached a rocky clearing with a few scattered evergreen trees. The view of the valley below was spectacular.

Martin pointed up to one of the trees. High above in the branches of the tree was the eagle's nest. It was huge—about the size of a child's treehouse.

Martin carefully climbed up another tree so he could get a better look inside the nest. He took some photographs and climbed down.

"Nothing," he said, disappointed.

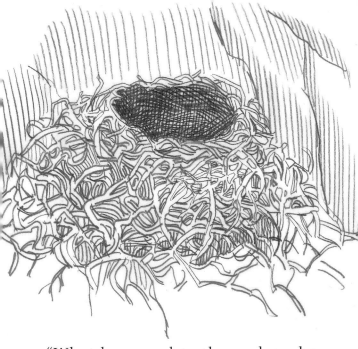

"What happened to the eagles who built it?" asked Philip.

"I don't know. Maybe they decided to build a new nest in a place where the hunting is better," Martin answered.

They started down a different route back to where the truck was waiting. About half way there they stopped at a stream. Martin unpacked some sandwiches. Esther and Philip took off their shoes and socks and dangled their toes in the ice-cold water as they ate.

After their picnic lunch, the trio continued down. Philip and Martin walked ahead of Esther, chattering away

about the eating habits of elk.

At a pause in the conversation, Esther heard a rustling. She still couldn't get thoughts of bears out of her mind. "What's that?" she asked in a shaky voice.

"I'm not sure," Martin said. He walked in the direction of the sound. Philip and Esther followed after him.

When they reached their cousin, he was leaning over a small animal tangled up in some kind of string.

"What is it?" asked Esther.

"It's a fox caught in a snare trap," Martin said angrily. The fox was scared and had a wild look in its eyes. Martin covered the fox with his jacket to protect himself from being bitten. Then he quickly cut the line. The frightened fox raced away.

Martin examined the knotted trap in his hand.

Philip picked up Martin's jacket

which the fox had dragged a few feet away. "Why would someone try to catch a fox?" Philip asked as he handed the jacket to Martin.

"Some people trap for food. Others trap for the animal's fur," Martin explained. "But it's illegal to trap on park land. That's called poaching. It's a serious crime."

By the time the trio got back to the truck it was almost three o'clock.

"Hop in," Martin said. "There's another nest I want to check. We have just enough time to get there." They all got into the truck.

Forty minutes later, they stood at the edge of a high cliff. "Don't get too close to the edge," Martin warned. "It could crumble under your feet."

Although she was still far from the edge, Esther took several steps back. Martin led them down to a narrow ledge on the side of the cliff.

"There," he said pointing to a nest resting on another rocky ledge. "I've been watching this nest for over a month now. When I first found it, there were already two eggs. The parent eagles took turns sitting on them to keep them warm. Later I watched one of the eggs hatch, and two days after

that, the other one hatched, too."

Philip leaned way over to get a better view of the baby birds.

"Philip! Be careful!" Esther warned. But she was too late. The rocks loosened beneath Philip's feet. He was sliding toward the edge!

Chapter Four

Esther screamed as she watched her brother teeter over the edge. In a flash, Martin swept his arm around Philip and pulled him in.

Martin handed over his binoculars to Esther. Then he sternly talked to Philip about safety rules.

Esther turned the binoculars towards the nest. It took a moment for her to adjust the focus. Then she saw the eaglets. "They're beautiful!" she said.

"Let me see," Philip demanded, trying to grab the binoculars from his sister.

"Wait a minute!" She elbowed him away. His near death had already escaped her mind.

"I almost forgot," Martin said as he took two smaller pairs of binoculars from his pack. "I bought these for you two. I knew it was the only way I'd be able to use my own this summer," he joked.

Philip and Esther used their new binoculars to study the eaglets. Even though Martin had said the eaglets had hatched within only two days of each other, there was no mistaking the oldest sibling. It was obviously bigger and stronger than the other one.

As they watched, an adult eagle landed in the nest. It started to feed the larger eaglet first.

"Hey! That's not fair," cried Philip.

"Shh!" whispered Esther.

Philip ignored his sister. "Martin, why doesn't the eagle feed the little bird first? It needs the food more."

"The parents always feed the largest

eaglet first. If there is enough food they'll feed the smaller one afterwards," Martin explained.

"But what if there isn't enough food?" asked Esther.

"Then the smaller eaglet starves," answered Martin.

Philip and Esther turned and looked at each other.

"It's lucky Mom and Dad aren't eagles! I would have starved to death a long time ago waiting for you to stop eating!" Philip poked his sister in the stomach.

Esther knocked Philip's hand away and turned to Martin. "Why do they let one eaglet starve when they could keep both alive with the food they have?"

"That's nature's way of deciding how many eaglets the land can support," Martin said. "When food is scarce, only one eaglet will survive. When there's lots of food, more can be raised."

They watched the older eaglet eat. It grabbed at small bits of food dangling from its parent's mouth.

Esther couldn't take her eyes off the little downy bird. As it finished all the food, Esther shifted her gaze to the smaller eaglet. She felt a pang of sadness.

Then she remembered the poachers. The animals the poachers took for themselves could have been food for the littlest eaglet. Her sadness turned to anger against the criminals who were stealing from the birds.

Back at the cabin that evening, Esther and Philip helped Martin prepare dinner on the fire they built outside. They grilled hamburgers and made popcorn. For dessert they roasted marshmallows over the hot coals.

Esther was tired after the day's hiking. She went into the cabin to brush her teeth. Then she went back outside to use the outhouse.

As she approached the outhouse she heard a low rumbling. At first, Esther thought it was a dog growling. "Wait, there aren't any dogs here," she thought as she felt a chill of fear run up her spine. She was just a few feet away from the outhouse door when she heard the

noise again. Now it sounded more like a deep roar . . . like a bear!

Just then the door of the outhouse burst open and something leapt out at her!

Esther screamed and covered her face with her hands.

"What's going on?" her cousin yelled as he came running around the corner

of the cabin. Esther opened her eyes and saw Philip rolling on the ground in front of her, laughing.

So the "bear" was her little brother—the little creep.

"Esther thought she heard a bear," Philip said between giggles.

Martin patted Esther on the shoulder and said good night.

Too embarrassed and angry to say anything, Esther stomped back into the cabin. "I'll get even with that little jerk," she said to herself.

Esther waited a whole week. Then, early one morning she got up quietly before Philip was awake. She found his binoculars and applied a thick wet coat of waterproof mascara around the rim of each lens.

"Philip!" she yelled loudly. "Look! It's a bear!"

Philip hopped out of bed and ran to the window where Esther was standing.

She passed the binoculars to him. "Quick! Look! Over there!" She pointed into the distance.

Philip put the binoculars to his face. "Where?" he asked looking out the window. "I don't see anything."

He took the glasses away from his face and Esther burst out laughing. Her little brother had dark circles around both his eyes, like a raccoon.

Martin came into the cabin to see what was going on. When he saw Philip, he burst into laughter, too.

During the next few weeks, Esther found herself relaxing into a routine. After breakfast, she and Philip would go with Martin to one of the nests he was observing. In the afternoon they'd go swimming in a nearby lake, or visit the ranger station where they read books and studied maps till dinner.

Sometimes Esther missed her friends and wondered what they were doing.

But most of the time she found herself
too caught up in her own adventure in
the wilderness to think about what she
was missing.

One morning, the threesome was
hiking to a nest about a mile away from
the cabin, when they heard a loud
screeching.

"That sounds like an eagle," Martin frowned. "But something's wrong." He raced towards the sound. Esther and Philip followed right behind him. They found an eagle caught in a snare trap.

Martin managed to free the eagle, and it flew off unharmed.

"Why would someone want to trap an

eagle?" asked Philip.

"I doubt that the poachers were trying to catch an eagle. But the eagle saw the bait and got caught in the trap," said Martin. He examined the snare. "This is the same type of fishing line that was used in the other trap we found. I'll bet it's the same poacher." Martin used his walkie talkie to report the incident to the ranger station.

"Do you think the rangers will catch the poacher?" asked Esther.

"Maybe," replied Martin. "But there's a lot of park land and only a few rangers. They can't police the entire area."

"Maybe we can catch the poachers," suggested Philip.

Martin shook his head. "Poachers are criminals, Philip," he said seriously. "Some of them carry guns and may be very dangerous. Leave it to the rangers."

Esther was outraged. Not only did the

poachers steal the eagles' food, they could also carelessly kill them. Well, this poacher wasn't going to get away with it—not if Esther could help it.

That evening at dinner, Martin told Esther and Philip he had to spend the next day in town working at the Wildlife Center's computers. "But you two can stay here and watch the eaglets, if you want," he said. "I'll leave the walkie talkie. If there's any problem, you can call the ranger station."

The next morning, Esther and Philip hiked to a nearby nest Martin had showed them earlier. Martin had set up a rope ladder in one of the trees so they could easily climb to a good viewing spot.

They watched the adult eagles feed their eaglets. Esther couldn't believe how much the little birds ate. She was fascinated by the whole process.

Eventually, the hungry eaglets made

Esther feel hungry and she glanced at her watch. It was afternoon already!

After a picnic lunch, Esther and Philip started back to the cabin.

"Look!" cried Philip, stopping in his tracks.

A rabbit had been caught in a snare

trap. Unlike the other trapped animals they had found, the rabbit hadn't survived. The line had choked it.

"Let's wait here and see if the poacher shows up," suggested Esther. They hid behind some thorny bushes nearby. But after about ten minutes, both Esther and Philip were restless.

"Stakeouts are more exciting on TV," complained Philip.

Esther had to admit that this wasn't her most brilliant idea. There was no way to know whether the poacher would come to check the trap that day.

But they might as well give it some time—and it was nice to sit down and rest. Esther settled back and found a comfortable position. She closed her eyes. The next thing she knew, Philip was shaking her awake. When she opened her eyes it was dark.

"Esther!" Philip shouted. "Wake up! We fell asleep! It's night!"

"Come on," said Esther. She took Philip's hand. "Let's hurry up and get back to the cabin."

But that was easier said than done.

Esther and Philip hadn't thought to bring a flashlight. Now the path, which was very clear in the daylight, had all but disappeared in the dark. After half an hour they knew they were lost.

"I guess I'd better use the walkie talkie," said Esther. But just as she lifted it from her pack, she saw a beam of light. Someone was walking toward them carrying a flashlight.

"It's the poacher!" cried Philip.

"Shhh!" Esther hissed. She remembered what Martin had said about poachers being dangerous criminals. She pulled Philip down beside her, trying to stay out of sight. But Philip lost his balance and fell noisily to the ground .

The flashlight beam turned in their direction.

"Uh, oh," whispered Philip.

The beam wavered, then found them, blinding Esther with its bright light.

Chapter Five

Just as Esther was about to spring and clobber the poacher with the walkie talkie, she heard a familiar voice. "Esther? Philip? Is that you?"

It wasn't the poacher. It was Martin!

"Hi," said Esther sheepishly. She and Philip stood up from behind the bush.

"What are you two doing out here?" asked Martin. "I was worried to death when I got back to the cabin and you weren't there."

"We found another snare. We were waiting to see if the poacher would come back," said Philip. "But then we fell asleep."

"I thought I told you . . ." Martin
paused. He took out his walkie talkie
and spoke into it: "Ranger station, I
found them. Thanks. Over and out."

Then he turned back to Esther and
Philip. "I tried calling you on my walkie
talkie. Didn't you hear me?"

"We didn't have ours turned on,"

admitted Esther.

"You two could have gotten hurt. Please don't try anything like this again," responded Martin.

Esther waited for his lecture, but Martin simply took Philip's hand and led them back to the cabin.

Martin didn't let his cousins out of his sight for the next two weeks.

Together, the three of them watched the eaglets in the different nests grow into young adults. Esther felt as if she knew each of the birds personally.

Soon it was time for Martin to begin banding the young eagles. Esther and Philip drove to the first nest with Martin and his partner, who had shown up for this particular task.

"Do the bands hurt the eaglets?" asked Philip in a worried voice.

"Nope," answered Martin.

Martin climbed up a tall evergreen tree to a nest high in its branches. He used a safety rope, but it still looked very dangerous from down below.

Martin carefully edged into the nest. An eagle perching nearby screeched loudly, startling Esther. Then the large bird flew over the nest.

Martin had said eagles rarely attack

52

the banders. Esther hoped this wasn't one of those occasions. The eagle circled, then landed on another branch.

Even though they couldn't see Martin very well, Esther and Philip knew exactly what he was doing. He had explained the banding process to them the previous evening.

First, he put a hood over the eaglet's head so it couldn't see. This calmed the bird. Next, he covered its claws so he wouldn't get scratched. He also wrapped the eaglet in a soft cloth to protect its wings. Then he gently put the bird into a large sack and lowered it to the ground.

There his partner recorded its size, its weight, and other important information. Finally, Martin's partner attached a numbered metal tag to the bird's leg. When that was done, the eaglet was returned to the nest. The whole process took about two hours.

Later, as the group was returning to the cabin that evening, Martin seemed more serious than usual. "This week, we're banding other eaglets all over the park," he said. "Since it's difficult work, I'd rather you two hang out around the cabin instead of with me."

"Don't worry, Martin," Esther said brightly. "We won't do anything stupid— like try to band a poacher!"

Martin smiled. "Promise?"

"Promise!" said Esther and Philip.

"Good. I'll leave a walkie talkie with you so you can call the ranger if you

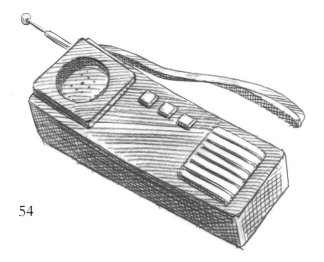

need anything."

The next day, Esther and Philip went to the nest near the cabin. They climbed up the rope ladder and settled in.

Esther focused her binoculars on the young eaglet in the nest. As she and Philip watched, an eagle flew to the nest and dropped a live fish inside. The fish flopped around and before the eaglet could spear it, the fish hopped right out of the nest.

Esther and Philip burst out laughing.

"I guess that's what you call a flying fish!" giggled Philip.

Esther turned her binoculars to see where the fish had fallen. Maybe the eagle would swoop down to get it.

But as she looked down to the ground she saw another movement farther down the hill. Somebody was crouched on the ground—setting a snare!

"Philip, look!" She nudged her brother. "It's the poacher!" Esther took

the walkie talkie from her pack to alert the rangers. But she was so nervous that she dropped it. The walkie talkie hit the ground below with a crash.

"Oh, no," cried Philip. "You broke it!"

"Shhh! Do you want the poacher to spot us? Come on!" said Esther. She scurried down the rope ladder.

"But we promised Martin we wouldn't try to catch the poacher," protested Philip, following behind.

"We won't try to catch him," said Esther. "We'll just take a picture of him so the rangers can identify him later!" Esther took her camera from her pack and hung it around her neck. Then she ran quickly but quietly down the hillside toward the poacher.

Chapter Six

Esther hid behind a tree a few yards away from the poacher. She looked through the camera and tried to frame the shot so the poacher's face was visible as he cut a piece of fishing line.

A branch was in the way. Esther tried to carefully bend it back, but it snapped off with a loud crack.

"Hey!" cried the poacher as he caught sight of her. "What are you doing?"

"I, uh, was taking pictures . . . of birds." Esther held up her camera.

Esther studied the poacher. He looked to be about her age, maybe a little younger. He still held the knife in one

hand. Its blade glistened in the afternoon sun.

Esther wondered if she could quickly take his picture then run. But Philip blew their cover.

"Why do you kill animals?" he accused the poacher. "Don't you know it's against the law?"

"Philip!" said Esther. "Let's just go."

"Wait a minute," said the poacher. His voice had turned menacing. "Who said I was killing animals? I was just trimming some line to go fishing with at the lake."

Esther knew he was lying, but she remembered her promise to Martin not to try to catch the poacher. She could identify him and let the rangers do their job.

"Besides," the poacher continued in a mean voice. "Who are you to tell me what to do? My family's been trapping animals in these woods for years and

years. We sell the pelts."

Just then, Esther heard the sound of heavy boots crunching against the forest floor. "What if it's another poacher?" Esther thought nervously. "How will Philip and I get away?"

"Esther! Philip!" Martin's voice carried through the woods.

"Over here!" shouted Philip. "Hurry! We caught the poacher!"

Martin came running before the poacher could get away.

An hour later the trio sat at the ranger station where they had taken the poacher. "How did you know where to find them?" the ranger asked Martin.

"I was worried when I couldn't reach them on the walkie talkie, so I went to the nest. I found the broken walkie talkie on the ground and looked around. It was lucky Philip was wearing a bright shirt or I never would have found them."

"What's going to happen to the poacher?" asked Esther.

"He's only fifteen, so he won't go to jail. But he'll have to do a lot of community service," said the ranger. He smiled at Martin. "Do you think you can handle him?"

"What do you mean?" asked Esther. She turned to Martin for an explanation.

"I agreed to take him on as an assistant," said Martin. "That way I can keep an eye on him. And maybe he'll learn how to help animals instead of hunting them."

Early in the morning before they had

to go home to the city, Philip's shouts woke Esther from a deep sleep. "Look, a bear!" he yelled.

"Try to be more original, Philip," Esther said as she rolled over in bed. She wanted to be well rested when she got home so she could tell her friends all about her exciting summer. She doubted any of her friends had ever even seen an eagle. And they'd never believe she actually helped catch a poacher!

"I'm not kidding, Esther! It's a real bear!" Philip persisted.

Esther figured she had better go along with Philip's joke if she wanted to get any more sleep that morning. So she sat up, looked outside, and saw a big, brown . . . bear!!

"I hope I'm dreaming," said Esther. And she soared back into bed, pulling the covers over her head.